TC, Key Lime Man

S.C. MacDorman

Special thanks to Nora Sloyan for her advice and encouragement, and to my husband, Walt, for indulging me.

ISBN: 978-0-578-00083-1

Cover Art by L.C. MacDorman
Back Cover Art by Louise Heywood

Recycle this book.

for Danny

Chapter 1

"Where've you been? You almost missed the bus."

Stevie dropped into the seat next to me. Normally I don't let him sit beside me, but I could tell something was really eating him.

"I was looking for my Flying Zork card," he said. "I stuck it inside my science book. Now it's gone."

I gathered that the Flying Zork was one of my brother's Mystic Zeltoid cards. Zeltoid cards are a big fad in Stevie's class right now. Practically every twerp has a deck of them.

"I bet Kenny swiped it," he said. Then he whipped around and glared in the general direction of the back of the bus. That's where Kenny usually sits.

Kenny Cravetz is this yob that lives down the street from us. He's got this wimpy nasal voice, and his nose is always running, even during the summer.

Coincidentally, the guy driving our bus is Kenny's next door neighbor. He isn't our regular bus driver, but he substitutes all the time. We all call him Uncle Rico, even though he's not our uncle. I noticed that Kenny didn't even say hi to him when he got on the bus. He's such a twit.

"I thought Kenny was into baseball cards," I said. Everyone knows about Kenny Cravetz's unbelievable baseball card collection. He brags about it all the time. How he has a 1952 Topps Mickey Mantle card that belonged to his uncle, along with a mint Cal Ripkin, Jr. (who doesn't?), two Brooks Robinsons, and a ripped Hank Aaron. What he brags about the most, though, is his Sandy Koufax, which he got from – get this – the Tooth Fairy.

The Tooth Fairy! Unbelievable.

The thing is, none of the kids Kenny's age give a crap about baseball cards. Most of them don't even know who Sandy Koufax is.

The Sandy Koufax card started a bunch of rumors around Stevie's class that the Tooth Fairy was actually their mothers. Kenny's card probably came from eBay, the kids said. Trouble was, none of the twerps who were spreading this rumor could prove anything.

Stevie decided he would be a big hero if he could somehow expose the Tooth Fairy for the fraud she was. He took the last five dollars she'd left him and used it to buy a fingerprinting kit. When the next tooth popped out two months later, he dusted TF's bill for fingerprints. To his astonishment, Stevie discovered that he was his own Tooth Fairy.

Big Hero.

Stevie stopped glaring at the back of the bus and was now transfixed on the seat in front of us. On the back of it someone had scribbled KOJAK SUCKS AN EGG with a blue marker.

As far as I know, no one at our school goes by the name Kojak. I do have my suspicions about a few of the kids who might actually suck eggs. Kenny Cravetz comes to mind.

When the bus got to our street, Uncle Rico drove past our usual stop and let us out right in front of our house.

"Thanks a lot, Uncle Rico," I said.

It pays to be nice to adults. A lot of kids act like jerks around them, but if you ask me, that's just stupid.

You never know when you might need one of them to give you a ride into town or keep a look out for you while you're toilet papering the Cravetz's front yard.

When we got off the bus, this big plaster fu dog was sitting on our front stoop staring us in the face.

"Yikes!" said Stevie. "Where did that come from?"

"It's a fu dog," I said, nudging my brother off the walkway. "It's the Chinese version of the sphinx."

"I know that," Stevie lied. "What's it doing on our step?"

"Protecting us from evil intruders," I said. "You'd better stay out here." I ran up the steps and locked Stevie out of the house.

I knew exactly where the fu dog had come from. "Nice statue," I said to my dad, who was sitting in his Lazy-Boy watching Court TV.

"Thanks."

From time to time, Dad picks up weird junk at work and brings it home. Not that he works any place particularly weird. He's the night watchman at a hotel downtown called the Shanghai.

Shanghai is the name of a city in China. It's also a word people sometimes use to mean kidnap. I guess that's a little weird.

Not a lot of people stay at the Shanghai anymore. The last time the place was full was during a Shriner's convention a couple of years ago. Dad brought home a bunch of those red fezzes with the tassels. That year for Halloween, Stevie and I dressed up as Egyptians.

A fez is a handy hiding place for a roll of toilet paper.

The Shanghai's management figured the reason the hotel is always vacant has something to do with the name of the place. As of last month, they officially changed it to the Saint George's.

Saint George supposedly slayed a dragon in England.

I guess now they'll put a dragon by the entrance.

The real reason most people stay away from the hotel is because it's a rat-trap. What it needs are a few cats.

"What happened to the other fu dog?" I asked my dad.

Fu dogs almost always come in pairs. There's even a proper way to place them around a door. Males on the right, females on the left, or vice versa, depending on whether you're coming or going.

Our dog was a male.

"The female fu was stolen," he said.

"You're kidding."

I opened the garage door and went outside to tell Stevie the news. "Somebody stole the other fu dog down at the Shanghai."

"Who'd want it?" said Stevie.

I shrugged. "Dad?"

Stevie followed me into the kitchen. "He's not a suspect, is he?"

I gave Stevie one of those older brother sneers. "Do you think anyone really cares?"

"Maybe he stole *that* one, too." Stevie nodded out the window toward the front stoop.

"Sure Stevie. Whatever you say."

"I'm going to find out where that other one is," he said.

"Maybe whoever took it has your Flying Zork card too," I said.

"Yeah, right."

Chapter 2

Stevie spent about fifteen minutes going up and down the block talking to people about the stolen fu dog. Most of the neighbors were already standing around outside watching Uncle Rico dig holes in his yard, so they were happy to take a few minutes to talk to Stevie. Of course, what they really wanted to talk about was Uncle Rico and what he was doing out there digging all those holes.

Most people thought he was either burying his winnings from the race track or looking for money he'd buried sometime before. A few speculated that he was trying to hide some sort of evidence from a crime scene. One kid thought he was burying a bunch of dead pets. Possibly gerbils.

Got to wonder what kind of crap is going on at that kid's house.

No one in our neighborhood knew anything about a missing statue from the Shanghai. They didn't even know it wasn't called the Shanghai anymore. So that was that.

Stevie did discover one interesting piece of information during his investigation, however, and that was that Kenny Cravetz was planning to break the record for watching the most consecutive hours of television. According to his sister, Belinda, Kenny was going to begin watching TV just as soon as school let out for summer vacation.

Stevie decided to go after the record too. I don't know if he was just doing it to stick it to Kenny because of the missing Flying Zork card, or whether he thought it was actually a good idea. You never know about Stevie.

To get a jump on Kenny, Stevie skipped the last day of school to stay home and watch television.

When Kenny found out that Stevie had beat him to the punch, he came over to our house and tried to break our TV by popping all the buttons off the control panel. He succeeded. Now you can't turn our television off.

When Kenny's mother found out what he'd done, she restricted him from TV for the entire summer.

Meanwhile, our television stayed on all summer. Unfortunately, it was permanently stuck on the Food Channel. After about three days, Stevie got bored and stopped watching.

So neither Stevie nor Kenny broke the record for consecutive hours of television watching, which actually belongs to a ninety-six year-old man who lives in a nursing home in South Bend, Indiana. He claims to have been staring at the tube since it was first invented. He was in his early thirties at the time.

One good thing came out of Stevie and Kenny's battle over the television. That summer, I became a gourmet cook.

Here's a cooking tip not many people have heard: while you're waiting for your dough to rise, suck an egg.

Gotcha!

Chapter 3

Here's another cooking tip – a real one this time: the most important ingredient in any recipe is the music you play while you're making it. Seriously. Tunes are the secret to good cooking.

Lately I've been listening to a lot of salsa music, for which my brother has been giving me a lot of crap. Not that Stevie dislikes salsa music so much. He's just kind of sick of eating things made from plantains.

I don't recommend fado music for cooking, unless of course you're making something like Portuguese peasant bread.

During that summer when I became a gourmet cook, Kenny Cravetz claimed that someone had stolen part of his baseball card collection, including his Mickey Mantle and his Sandy Koufax.

Poor, nasal-nose Kenny, I said.

Then the next day, somebody pinched a loaf of Portuguese peasant bread, which I'd left cooling on the front step by the fu dog.

The secret ingredient of peasant bread, by the way, is baby cereal. When I told Stevie this, he said that it was gross and he wasn't going to eat it anymore.

Sometimes there's no pleasing Stevie.

Then again, Stevie can be a real moron.

He tells his friends that I poison our food. It started when the entire family became violently ill after one of my meals. It was weiner schnitzel with a side of buttered spaetzle. They all said it was food poisoning. Even Mom.

Later, Dad remembered that one of the hotel guests had coughed on him. He said that maybe he'd picked up a virus down at the Shanghai. More than likely.

A few days after Kenny's baseball cards and my loaf of bread were stolen, the police found the thief holed up in a rest room at the back of the Gas 'n Go. Some old dude.

It was a miracle that they found him back there. Nobody ever uses the rest room at the Gas 'n Go – not since World War II, which was the last time it was cleaned.

The only reason they found the guy was because there was smoke coming out from under the bathroom door. The old dude had set fire to Kenny's baseball cards.

Mickey Mantle was toast.

They discovered the old man kneeling in front of the toilet, clutching a half-eaten loaf of Portuguese peasant bread.

The police said he must have gone insane from the rest room fumes. He was all twitchy and murmuring weird stuff like, "DON'T SAY *UK*, MY FICKLE AXE-MAN!"

Not all of Kenny's cards were damaged in the fire. Sandy Koufax, it seems, had been flushed.

Later the police figured out that it was actually my bread that made the old guy go crazy. The bread, it turns out, was laden with LSD.

"What did I tell you?" said Stevie.

Just to clear things up, I did not purposely lace that loaf with LSD. Besides, it wasn't actually LSD, but a fungus called ergot, which just happens to be the same stuff that LSD is made out of.

After a thorough investigation of the crime scene, the police traced the source of the fungus to a farmers' market downtown. Dad sometimes stops there in the morning on his way home from work. A few weeks ago he bought a sack of unthreshed wheat there. He thought it was something I might be able to use now that I'm a gourmet cook.

Not a lot of recipes call for unthreshed wheat. I had to improvise a bit with the Portuguese peasant bread.

Some historians claim that ergot poisoning was what turned all those girls into witches back in 1692 Salem. The fungus caused them to have hallucinations. Naturally they acted kind of strange. As a result, those poor out-of-their-mind witches were stoned to death.

Stoned for the crime of eating bad bread.

Sheesh.

Stevie was very curious to know what I'd done with the rest of the hallucinogenic wheat.

"What do you care?" I asked.

"Come on, Finch. Just tell me."

Everyone calls me Finch. My real name is Atticus, after the character Atticus Finch in *To Kill a Mockingbird*. My mother went into labor during a Gregory Peck film festival. If I'd been born a girl, she'd have probably named me Scout – you know, the name of Gregory Peck's character's daughter.

"I chopped it all up and tossed it in your cereal this morning. Pretty soon you should start feeling imaginary bugs crawling all over your skin."

"Cut it out, Finch."

Why couldn't she have just named me Gregory?

"Where'd you really put it?"

"I scattered it over by the duck pond."

"Seriously?"

"Check it out yourself if you don't believe me." I pointed out the back window toward the duck pond.

Stevie nearly wet his pants. "Holy crap!" he said.

"What, never seen a flock of ducks flying upside down before?"

Chapter 4

The old bum who stole my bread recovered a week later. The townspeople felt so bad about his being poisoned, they convinced the mayor that it was the town's civic duty to look after him. So the mayor arranged for him to have free housing.

Guess where he's living?

In a room at the Saint George's.

"I bet he's the one who stole their fu dog," said Stevie.

"So where is it now?" I asked.

"How should I know? Probably stashed it in another gas station toilet."

Anything's possible.

Since the old dude doesn't have a job or anything to keep him busy, he spends most of his time loafing around the hotel doing word puzzles. Dad says he's also a pretty good card player.

My father's got to have one of the easiest jobs in the world.

One evening when Dad didn't have to work, he invited the thief over to our house for dinner. Check this out – his name is Scout. Wonder where his mother was when she went into labor.

Actually, Scout is just a nickname the old dude picked up in Mexico. According to my father, he used to work for some baseball franchise, where his job was to travel to all these remote villages south of the border and search for new talent. His real name, Dad said, was Eddie the Aztec.

Talking to Scout is a bit of a challenge. Ever since the baseball card fire, he speaks only in phrases made by rearranging the letters in the names of his two favorite baseball players, Sandy Koufax and Mickey Mantle.

The only time Scout's really lucid is when he's telling baseball stories from the old days. Then he speaks in more or less normal sentences. The rest of the time it's Sandy Koufax-Mickey Mantle anagrams.

For instance, when I served a plate of smoked salmon appetizers, he stood up and exclaimed, "TAX DICEY! MAKE FUNKY SALMON!"

"I think that means he likes it," said Dad.

I could see that. The old dude gorfed down the entire tray's worth by himself.

There is a surprising number of phrases that can be made out of the names of two baseball players. From just Mickey Mantle alone you can make MELT IN MY CAKE, MANY TICKLE ME and T–MEN CLAIM KEY.

Here's one Scout blurted out upon spotting a stack of Stevie's comic books on the coffee table: A LUCKY DAY. X-MEN SMOTE A FINK!

Scout had a lot of interesting stories about his days in baseball. Once when he was working for the Mexican City Red Devils, he had to fight a bull just to secure a contract for a short stop.

Red Devils are what Hernando DeSoto used to call the Native Americans back in the 1540s when he was plundering their land. Ever since then, we think of Satan as this little red guy with horns and a trident. Before then, most people probably just imagined him looking like Gregory Peck.

Personally, I like to picture Satan looking like Hernando DeSoto. The trident would still suit him, since his body was fed to the catfish at the bottom of the Mississippi River.

For some reason I think of tridents every time I use those little forks for fondue, even though most fondue forks have two tines, not three.

Tines.

Not a word you hear a lot these days.

I thought about making fondue the night Dad brought Scout home, but instead I fixed a cheese soufflé. It was all puffed up and golden brown when I pulled it from the oven. Then Stevie came running into the kitchen all charged up about the bull fight story and screamed, "Toro! Toro!" Then he picked up a butter knife and gored my soufflé.

It caved in like Belinda Cravetz's chest.

"Jerk."

Did you know that a long time ago, the Devil supposedly made the rounds on Christmas Eve with Santa? Maybe that's why Santa always wears red. Maybe he's actually possessed by the Devil. SANTA – SATAN. Think about it.

Scout didn't seem to care about the big sink hole in my soufflé. He had three helpings. Number of poppy-seed muffins: zero.

When I brought out the pie for dessert, Scout grinned at me and said in a cool Latino voice, "TC, KEY LIME MAN!"

It was actually lemon meringue. Close enough.

I noticed when Scout grinned he had a gold tooth. It made him look kind of like a pirate.

After dinner he showed us a couple of card tricks. Instead of saying, "Pick a card," he'd say something like, "Y EXAMINE A MOLDY SKUNK FACT?" Or "MAD UNCLE KAY MAKES TINY FOX."

Then when he'd reveal the card you'd picked, he'd shout, "MY FAKE TOXIC LAND SNAKE! YUM!"

He was really good at card tricks. You'll never believe what card he pulled from behind my brother's ear – the Flying Zork. Stevie's bottom jaw dropped like a broken elevator.

Scout pointed a finger at himself and winked. "YUKKY, MEAN OLD MEXICAN FAST!"

After he left, I decided to try one of his tricks. Guess what? He stole our deck of cards.

I went back into the kitchen to clean up the dinner dishes. I threw the leftover poppy-seed muffins out to the ducks.

I'm thinking that Scout was probably whacked-out long before the baseball card fire.

Chapter 5

One of the ducks flew down our chimney. They've been acting weird ever since I tossed out the wheat. Stevie suggested that we start a fire and smoke it out.

I actually do have a recipe for smoked duck with plum sauce. I found it on a website for Asian cooking, right under the recipe for dog stew.

According to the website, dogs used in stew are not pets. No kidding.

The fu dog is really more like a lion than a dog.

Scout was very enthusiastic about our statue from the Shanghai. He stopped to rub its head before he entered the house.

"Is that for luck?" my father asked.

"ASK ANDY FU-OX," said Scout.

Now we all refer to the statue as Andy.

"I still think he's got the other one," said Stevie.

"You mean, Ann?"

Stevie gave me an annoyed sideways glance and walked out of the room, though I don't think it had anything to do with my fu dog comment. Most likely he just wanted to snag the last cream soda before I could get it.

When summer rolled around again, my father got me a job cooking at the Saint George's. The new English pub they'd put in to replace the Chinese restaurant had turned out to be a bust.

Who would have thought?

It was pretty easy for Dad to convince the hotel's management that his kid's cooking couldn't be any worse than the crappy fish and chips they'd been serving for the last twelve months. It helped that I came so cheap.

I was a little nervous that first day, but Dad told me not to worry about it.

"Nobody eats here anyway," he said. "Except of course for Scout and me."

That evening I made roast duck. Dad looked a little freaked out when I set it on the table.

"That's not..."

"Nah," I said. "It's not Zork."

Zork is the name of Stevie's pet duck – the same duck that got stuck in our chimney. Stevie managed to coax it out with my leftover lemon meringue pie. Now the dumb bird lives with us.

"This one came from the farmers' market down the street," I told Dad.

Dad's expression morphed from freaked out to something closer to concern. "I thought they shut that place down, you know, after the wheat."

"It just re-opened." I carved off a piece of breast and put it on his plate. "Have some."

He looked at his watch. "Why don't you wrap that up for me to eat later. I really need to get back to my post."

His post was a leather armchair across the lobby.

Whatever.

I wasn't surprised by my father's reaction to the duck. He's not really into gamey foods.

Scout, on the other hand, said it was the best thing he'd ever tasted. His exact words were, "YO! A FINE DUCK, MY MAN, T. ASK LEX."

It's nice to prepare a meal for someone who appreciates your cooking.

I asked Scout if he'd like to help me out in the kitchen sometime. He flashed me the gold tooth and said, "MAD YAKS EXCEL AT FUNNY MOIK." Then he flipped a spoon into the air and caught it in his shirt pocket.

I have no idea what that was supposed to mean.

"What it means is, he's a freakin' thief," Stevie said the next day when I told him about it.

That gave me an idea.

I took out a piece of paper and wrote the names of Scout's two favorite baseball players at the top of it.

MICKEY MANTLE ... SANDY KOUFAX

Then I tried to recall as many of his quirky anagrams as I could, and I wrote them down. After that I tried making up a few of my own. It's harder than you think. In three hours, I'd only managed to come up with five or six phrases.

Using just the letters of Mickey Mantle's name, I made two: ME KC – TINY MALE and Y KNIT ME CAMEL?

The better anagrams came from Sandy Koufax: SKY OF XANADU and U ASK FOXY DAN.

My best one came from the combination of both names: FAUSTIAN MONKEY LACK X-Y MED.

"Who the heck is Foxy Dan?"

Stevie had sneaked into my room to spy on me. I can't believe I didn't hear him come in with that stupid duck in his arms.

"None of your business," I said.

To be honest, I had no idea what any of these weird sayings were supposed to mean. At least, not yet. Assigning specific meanings to each anagram was the next step in my plan.

My idea was to translate Scout's word-scramble language into real English. It would be sort of like a lexicon for all the weird jumbled-up word-phrases.

I thought the first thing that I should establish in our new language were names for us to call each other. Since there was no way to make either the words Finch or Atticus out of Mickey Mantle-Sandy Koufax, I thought I'd tell him to call me TC, KEY LIME MAN. I liked the sound of it. It was kind of catchy.

If he wanted to refer to himself, I would suggest he use the phrase MANY–A–MEX FAN LIKED SCOUTY K.

That was another one of mine. The K doesn't really mean anything. Sometimes you just end up with a leftover letter or two when you're rearranging the names of famous ball players.

I'm not really sure what Scout's last name is. I somehow doubt it's "The Atzec." Who knows? Maybe it's Klingerhoffer or Kilgore or something like that.

Stevie set the duck on top of my head. "You can make a few dirty words out of that, you know."

I knew.

"Get that stupid duck off my head." I waved my hand in the air. "I don't want it crapping on me."

That's the worst part about having a duck for a pet – all the crap everywhere.

I tried to rearrange the letters of Mickey Mantle and Sandy Koufax to come up with something about duck crap. Unfortunately, I lacked the necessary R and P. Nor did I have an H for the other four-letter word commonly used to refer to crap.

Instead I left this note on Stevie's bed that night: F*** YE, YA DAMN LAME STINK-OX!

I was risking getting in some serious trouble with Mom using the F-bomb, though technically I didn't actually use it. I let Stevie fill in the blanks with the only three remaining letters.

He came down for breakfast the next morning wearing a dopey grin.

"What do you want for breakfast?" I asked.

"Corn pops, ya damn lame stink-ox."

Ever since that day, the phrase "ya damn lame stink-ox" has been our code for flipping each other off. By the end of the summer, it had boiled down to simply "stink-ox."

"Did you swipe my cream soda?"

"Stink-ox."

"Stink-ox, yourself."

Chapter 6

Scout was waiting for me in the kitchen that afternoon when I got to work. I could tell he was very excited about something by the way he was playing the spoons on his thigh.

Not everyone has a knack for playing the spoons. Scout was pretty good. His slapping was intense. The beat kind of reminded me of salsa music.

Scout likes my salsa music, though I get the feeling that the Latin rhythms make him a little homesick for Mexico.

"You're in a good mood," I said.

Scout clanged his spoons on a couple of pots hanging over the stove. Then he jumped up to help me with my bag of groceries.

"Thanks." I took a step back when Scout started pulling things out of my bag. He was very interested to see what I'd bought. The way he ripped into it reminded me of the way Stevie goes after a Christmas gift.

Last Christmas Stevie was all upset because Dad had made a fire in the fireplace. He was worried that Santa wouldn't be able to get down the chimney.

"Satan doesn't care about fire, you twerp. He lives in Hell, for God's sake."

My mother shot me a sharp look. "Atticus, would you please stop telling your brother that Santa Claus is possessed by the Devil?"

"Whatever," I said.

When Stevie went to bed that night, I cut out a couple of cardboard horns and taped them onto my fez. Then I sneaked outside and walked in the shadows by Stevie's window saying, "Ho Ho Ho."

He totally freaked.

Speaking of freaked, Scout looked a little twitchy when he finished emptying my grocery bag. He squinched his eyes all up, which made his eyebrows a little slanty looking. If he'd been wearing the fez, he'd almost look like the Devil.

"NO MAKE ANY DUCK FILETS, MAXY?" he said.

I think he meant FILLET and not one of those little mesh squares. Then again, he might have been speaking in French.

"No," I said. "No duck tonight."

He picked up a spoon and smacked a pan. The sound rang in my ear. Now *I* was beginning to get a little freaked.

"Sorry Scout. I was planning on having pot roast."

Scout shook his head.

"You don't like pot roast?"

He clanged the pot again. It was beginning to get irritating. I wish I knew what his problem was with pot roast.

Then I remembered the lexicon. I pulled it out of my shirt pocket and laid it on the counter in front of him.

His expression relaxed a little.   His eyebrows smoothed out into a pair of sleeping caterpillars suspended above his brown eyes. He actually looked impressed with my work.   After studying it for a minute or two, he pointed to an expression I'd heard him use at our house when I was making the soufflé.

"UK EXTOL SICK DAME, FANNY MAY!"

Since I had no idea what he'd meant the first time he'd said it, I made up my own definition. In my lexicon it means *Look at her! Doesn't she make you sick?*

Wow. Something was really eating him. Unfortunately, I still had no idea what it was. So much for the dumb lexicon.

"You know, I could make you a sandwich or something. You don't have to eat the pot roast."

He shook his head and banged another pot.

I wish he'd quit doing that.

I started gathering up my knives and pans and onions and junk that I needed to prep my roast. It wasn't that I didn't want to talk to Scout, I just really needed to get going on the evening's meal.

Scout began pacing back and forth in front of the stove, which can be kind of a nuisance when you're trying to cook. I didn't know what to say. I stink at stuff like that, even when I can understand the other person's language. All I could think to do was put on my apron and start chopping onions.

Scout marched out of the kitchen.

At least now I could get to the stove. I turned it on to heat it up and continued with my chopping. I felt like I was chopping onions for hours. Luckily, I know the trick about stuffing a piece of bread in your mouth, so I didn't cry or anything.

Even though my eyes didn't water, the rest of me was drenched. I was sweating like a pig in that old kitchen. Just because the place has a new name, it doesn't mean it isn't the same old rat-trap of a hotel. The kitchen has no ventilation at all, so all the heat from the oven just hangs in the air. Kind of like smog in LA, except that smog actually smells better than the air in that place.

Because it has no place to go, the air in that place holds every stinking smell that's ever been generated in that kitchen over the past fifty years.

Eggroll smells.

Fried fish smells.

Some old cook's fart.

The place reeks like a garbage truck.

Makes you hungry, doesn't it?

The chopping was giving me carpal tunnel syndrome, I think. If Scout came back, I might ask him to help me out. Unless he's still acting twitchy. As a rule, twitchy people shouldn't really be doing a lot of junk with knives. Spoons were bad enough.

While I was chopping, I noticed that my lexicon was gone. Scout must have taken it with him. I was glad I'd left out the STINK-OX phrase. He probably wouldn't have cared, but you have to watch it a little with older people. Dad wouldn't care, not really. He'd only pretend to care, to go along with Mom.

Mom would cream me.

Once when my mom was at the store, Dad busted the lawn mower when he ran over a rock. I heard him say at least four bad words in a row, including the F-bomb.

The next year, Stevie was put in charge of cutting our lawn. You'd think Dad would have put me in charge since I'm older, but when I was little I had allergies, so now I never have to do anything like that. Sweet.

I looked at the clock. It was already quarter to four. Technically, the dining room opened for dinner at five-o-clock. If I didn't get that roast in the oven soon, I'd have to change the menu to stir fry.

It was a lot more work cooking for an entire restaurant than for just Mom, Dad and Stevie. Not that I was actually feeding a whole restaurant's worth of people, but I had to be ready just in case.

Just when my arm was about to fall off, Scout burst through the door.

"DUCK SNAFU OKAY!" Which was really written DX SNAFU OKAY. I suppose the letters DX kind of sound like DUCK.

SNAFU is actually an old acronym from World War I or II, I can't remember which. Nobody uses it very much anymore. It stands for SITUATION NORMAL – ALL F***ED UP.

There's that F-bomb again. Mom said if she ever hears Stevie or me say it, she'll cut out our tongues.

Nice way to talk to your kids.

I hadn't changed the DUCK SNAFU expression too much when I'd translated it for my lexicon. It basically meant that everything was okay, more or less.

"Great," I said.

Scout shot me the tooth. Then he handed me a piece of hotel stationary. On it he'd written the words NO-FAT DUCK, YEN YAMS, KALE MIX.

"Yen yams?"

The tooth was still glinting at me.

"Are you telling me this is what you want for dinner?"

Scout nodded.

"How 'bout I make that for you tomorrow?" I said, assuming I could figure out what the heck a yen yam was.

He shook his head and handed me another piece of stationary. On it were written the exact same words: NO-FAT DUCK, YEN YAMS, KALE MIX.

That's when I noticed he was holding a whole stack of hotel stationary, and every page had the same thing written on it.

That confirms it. Scout's a psycho. Like that *Here's Johnny* guy in the movie *The Shining*.

"Why do you have so many?" I asked. I tried not to act all freaked out just because he was acting like a psycho. Anyway, I was the one holding the knife.

Scout began to pantomime as if he were handing out stationary to people walking by.

"Scout?" I said.

He stopped.

"Are you trying to tell me that you've been passing these things out to people?"

He had.

"Okay," I said, but what I thought was SNAFU.

Chapter 7

I'm toast.

There's no way I could prepare a duck dinner before five-o-clock.

I checked the refrigerator. My father's leftover duck was still on the shelf sitting next to my cream soda. No surprise there. That at least gave me something to work with. I know it's pretty lame to serve reheated water fowl for the evening meal, but sometimes you don't have much choice.

Tonight's special: lame duck.

With a side of pot roast.

I slapped the meat into the oven and sent Scout out to the market for sweet potatoes and kale. Never mind getting any more duck. I'd never have time to prep it and cook it through before five.

I did have time to whip up some yen yams, however, which I decided was just a fancy way of saying sweet potato tempura.

If I bombed as a chef, I could get a job making up definitions for weird sayings.

Kale mix: stir-fried greens and onions.

Lots of onions.

With a little rice vinegar and soy sauce, I'd have a whole Japanese dinner going.

Scout was back in a flash. I set him to work peeling potatoes. He was a champion potato peeler. He finished up the whole sack in about fifteen minutes.

About quarter to five the kitchen door swung open. It was Faarooq, Dad's boss.

"How's it going, Saheeb?"

When I spoke of hotel management earlier, I was referring to Faarooq. He and his wife actually own the hotel. Her name is Ba-Boo or Bubba or something like that. I don't ever actually speak to her, so it doesn't really make much difference to me what her name is.

Faarooq sniffed the air. "More duck?" As if he could actually smell something besides garbage truck in there. I hope he didn't think it was my cooking.

"Yeah," I said. "More duck."

Faarooq and Boo-Boo are strict vegetarians. Dad said they never ate dinner in the hotel dining room.

Last night I didn't see Faarooq until I was walking out the door to leave, around ten-thirty or so. He'd come down to the lobby to get a few magazines.

I think I'm the only person who actually does any work in that place. I don't even think anyone cleans the rooms. There's no need. No one ever stays in them.

"How much for duck?" asked Faarooq, giving the air another sniff.

I was supposed to keep a record of what I spent on food for the restaurant, but I hadn't quite gotten around to organizing a system yet.

"I think it was about five dollars a pound," I guessed.

Faarooq shook his head. "Not how much cost," he said. "How much charge?"

"How much charge?"

"On menu. What we charge for No-Fat Duck?"

I shrugged. "Ten bucks?" Even after the yen yams and kale mix, that would still leave a decent profit.

Faarooq shook his head. "Sixteen-fifty," he said. Then he gave a little bow and left.

Scout was grinning with that gold tooth of his. He gave me the thumbs-up sign. Then he picked up a pair of spoons and started slapping everything in sight.

For sixteen-fifty, I should probably make more duck sauce. With enough sauce you can kill the taste of anything. Even leftover water fowl.

I was working like a demon, trying to ignore the banging spoons in the background, when I heard voices on the other side of the door. They didn't belong to either Dad or Faarooq. Definitely not Bubba, even though I didn't know what she sounded like.

"Wonder who's out there," I said.

Scout stopped playing.

That helped.

He darted over to the door and pushed it open a crack.

The tooth flashed.

He closed the door and banged a pot.

"Well?"

"I'M ANDY K. LACKY, NEXUS TO FAME!"

Chapter 8

Turns out, Andy K. Lacky had passed out more than five-hundred pieces of stationary that afternoon. That's twice as many pieces of stationary as there are people in the whole town.

At ten minutes to five there was a line in front of the Saint George's stretching all the way down the block to the farmers' market. At least a hundred people were outside waiting for half a leftover duck and something called yen yams. I wondered where they all came from.

"New Jersey, more than likely," said Dad.

Faarooq blew back into the kitchen. He was wearing one of those small aprons that waiters sometimes wear. He sniffed.

"Duck ready?"

"Since last night," I said.

Faarooq smiled. He never showed any teeth when he smiled, but I doubt any of his were gold.

"Nineteen-ninety-nine a plate," he said.

"I thought you said sixteen-fifty?"

"Now nineteen-ninety-nine." He gave a little bow. "Plus tax and tip." Before he slipped back out through the swinging door, he threw a second little apron to Scout.

"Big game today, Mr. Aztec."

Scout flipped his wrist over like a baseball player and snagged that apron out of the air as if he were fielding a line drive. It almost looked like he was wearing a baseball glove the way he clamped his fingers around the apron. I must have been staring at him with a strange expression, because he winked at me.

"I always had an eye for talent," he said, just as normal as you please. Then he wrapped the apron around his waist and followed Faarooq into the dining room.

Only four people actually ate duck that night. The other ninety-six had pot roast lathered in plum sauce. I don't think anyone knew the difference. If they did, they didn't say anything.

After thinking it over, only seventy-three people had the pot roast. The other twenty-three got tired of waiting and had a picnic in the parking lot at the market. The guy who runs the place set up tables in front of his vegetable carts and gave everyone free chips and salsa.   The salsa was a homemade mixture with tons of hot chili peppers.

Everyone's mouth was on fire.

The market guy charged five bucks for a bottle of water.

The market guy is smarter than he looks.

He looks like a roadie for a punk band. He has all these tattoos and spiky hair that's dyed orange. He's got a ring in his nose, and one of his ears is pierced. The other ear looks like someone took a bite out of it.

Not to sound judgmental, but the guy's basically a freak. I try not to look directly at him when I'm buying something there. Same rule you'd apply to the sun.

It's funny how if you put something out like really hot salsa, and one person tastes it and says, "Man, this is so hot," or more likely he screams, "WATER!" suddenly everyone wants to try the stuff to see if it's really as hot as the guy whose mouth is on fire says it is. And of course it is.

People can be so dumb.

Why else would seventy-seven people wait in line for NO-FAT DUCK, YEN YAMS and KALE MIX.

By the time I finished cleaning up that night, it was after midnight. I'd missed the last bus home.

Faarooq said it was okay for Dad to leave his post to drive me back to our house. He and Bubba were sitting at one of the dining room tables counting their money.

Scout was still up too. I saw him plop himself down in Dad's armchair as we walked out the door. He was working on one of his word puzzles.

He really is a whiz at those things. He does them in pen. Usually a permanent blue marker.

I was really tired when I got home, but I couldn't get to sleep. In my head I was still chopping and stirring and frying and junk.

When I finally did fall asleep, I dreamed that I accidentally stir-fried Zork. I woke up in a sweat, so I decided to get some water. As I got out of bed, I stepped in a fresh pile of duck crap.

Chapter 9

Last night while Dad was driving me home, somebody tried to rob the Saint George's.

That's what happens when you don't have any fu dogs guarding your door.

The only thing that sits in front of the hotel these days is a potted plant, which is pretty much dead. Most people think it's just an ashtray.

According to Faarooq, a guy wearing a cowboy hat and a purple mask walked into the place after Dad and I left. He walked right past Scout, who was into his word puzzle and not really paying attention to who was coming and going.

Not that anyone besides Dad and me would either come or go at that hour.

The masked cowboy headed straight for the dining room. He asked Faarooq if he would be so kind as to give him the money they were counting. Then he started waving this long blackish thing at Boo-boo.

According to Faarooq, the thing the guy was waving didn't look very much like a gun. What it looked like, he said, was one of those Oriental eggplants.

"Why are you waving an eggplant at my wife, Saheeb?"

Saheeb is the name Faarooq calls anybody whose name he doesn't know.

The masked guy in the hat didn't answer, though he did stop waving around the eggplant.

Then Bubba whispered something to Faarooq in Hindi.

"What did she say?" asked the cowboy with the eggplant.

"She said there is a lot of loose change here. She said I should go find a bag to put it in."

"Oh," said the Eggplant Cowboy.

Faarooq gave a little bow and went into the kitchen, leaving the guy with the eggplant standing over his wife at the dining room table.

It's not exactly clear what happened next, since neither Ba-boo nor Scout really says much. All I know is, when Faarooq returned with the empty potato sack, he found the cowboy sitting at the table playing poker with Scout.

Bubba had scooped most of the money into the lap of her sari and gone to her room. She'd given Scout and the masked cowboy each a couple of quarters to use in their poker game.

By the time Dad got back to his post, the intruder had left, and Faarooq had gone to bed. Only Scout was still hanging around, sitting in Dad's big leather armchair flipping quarters off his elbow and catching them in his hand.

That Scout has quick hands.

Dad went into the kitchen to grab a snack. Of course, there wasn't a thing to eat in that smelly place. The dinner crowd had wiped me out of just about everything, including onions.

The only thing he could find to eat was an Oriental eggplant. He fried it up and ate it. Then he fell asleep over the sink and dreamed he was driving a garbage truck through New Jersey.

Chapter 10

"I bet that Eggplant Cowboy's got the other fu dog," said Stevie when Dad told us what happened.

"Give it a rest, Stevie," I said. I was pretty tired after feeding seventy-seven people. I really didn't give a rip about the other fu dog.

But Stevie was all geared up to re-open the case. He begged Dad to let him come downtown with us so he could start looking for clues.

Dad said it was all right with him if Stevie came.

I think Stevie was more interested in finding the identity of the Eggplant Cowboy than he was about finding the missing fu dog, but he didn't admit it. He knew that if he said he was going directly after an armed bandit, everyone would tell him it was too dangerous.

It would definitely sound a lot more impressive to say you'd nailed the guy who tried to hold up a hotel than to say you found some dumb old lost statue of a Chinese lion.

Like always, we stopped at the market on the way to the hotel. Stevie nudged me and pointed to a basket of Oriental eggplants. He said it was a major clue.

I told him that lots of places sell eggplant, but he was convinced that the punk rocker who runs the market was really the masked cowboy.

I have to admit, the guy at the market is a little weird.

Then again, who isn't?

I was thinking of a seafood special for tonight, even though the fish at the market aren't as fresh as some of the other stuff you can get there. That's kind of understandable since we don't live anywhere near the water. Unless you consider the duck pond behind our house, water.

I was wavering between poached salmon with lemon and a nice grilled sea bass, when I noticed a special on catfish. Barbecued catfish. I was psyched.

But Stevie said he wouldn't eat anything that had whiskers like that. It would be too much like eating Uncle Rico.

All the kids love Uncle Rico. Even though he's a grown up, he doesn't really act like one. He does goofy stuff like a kid would do, like burying money in his front lawn. And he never combs his hair. It's always sticking out every which way, just like his mustache. I guess he does kind of look like a catfish.

One of the main reasons the kids love Uncle Rico is because he gives out sodas on Halloween.

The Cravetzes always hand out terrible candy for Halloween, like lemon taffy and chocolate covered raisins.

Last year they gave out toothbrushes.

Toothbrushes!

When Stevie got his toothbrush from them, he decided to egg their house. But when he came home to get the eggs, I was cooking an omelet.

"Why don't you just toilet paper the place?" I said.

"We've already done that," he said. The truth was, Stevie didn't have a very strong arm. He was probably afraid he couldn't lob the rolls high enough to clear the tree branches. Last year I did most of the work. Stevie was pretty useless.

"If you wait until I'm done eating, I'll help you," I said. I wasn't really in the mood to TP a house right then. It was kind of cold outside. But I figured it was for a good cause.

"Nah," said Stevie. "I've got a better idea." Then he grabbed a bunch of plastic forks out of the pantry and planted them all over the Cravetz's lawn. I'm not sure what the point of that was, but Stevie thought it was pretty hilarious.

It made me think of that word, tines.

I imagined Mr. Cravetz looking out the window saying, "Look at all those tiny tines poking out of the ground."

Of course, he'd never say anything like that. He'd just make Kenny go out and pull them all up, just like he'd made him clean up the toilet paper.

Mr. Cravetz assumes that it's because of Kenny that people do stuff to his house, which is basically true.

Kenny knew it was Stevie who'd stuck all those forks in his grass. There aren't a whole lot of other twerps around who'd do something like that besides Stevie. Or him.

The kid with the dead gerbil fixation was still too young for those types of pranks, though he would definitely be a contender in a few years.

Uncle Rico might plant forks in his own lawn, but never in anyone else's.

The next day at school, Kenny stuck a chocolate bar between the pages of Stevie's science book.   Stevie showed it to me on the bus home.

"What are you going to do?" I asked.

"I'm not sure yet," he said.

"Why don't you smear something on the inside of his book?" I very thoughtfully suggested.

"Like what?"

"How 'bout some duck crap."

"Good idea."

We spent the rest of the ride home staring in silence at the words KOJAK SUCKS AN EGG on the seat in front of us, which incidentally, is now my permanent seat on the bus.

Chapter 11

Stevie had insisted on bringing Zork to the hotel the afternoon he began snooping around for the Eggplant Cowboy. I can't believe my father let him. I'm sure Bubba and Faarooq don't want duck crap all over their hotel.

"He's trained," said Stevie.

"Yeah, right," I said. "Just don't let him in my kitchen or I'll cook him."

Stevie sat in the dining room and played cards with Scout while I got to work on my dinner. I finally settled on bouillabaisse. I put on an old Miles Davis CD to set the mood. Bouillabaisse is one of those freestyle dishes that allows for lots of improvisation, just like jazz.

I was rinsing off some clams when Stevie came running into the kitchen. I remember what happened the last time he got talking to Scout just before dinner. I stepped in front of the pot on the stove to block him from doing anything stupid like he'd done with my cheese soufflé. Not that you can really do much to bouillabaisse.

Stevie shoved me aside and grabbed the lid off the pot. "Whad'ya do with Zork?" he cried.

"I didn't do anything with that stupid duck. Get away from my bouillabaisse."

Even if you spit in it, nobody would know the difference.

"Zork's gone."

I figured that. "Maybe Faarooq did something to him because of the duck crap," I said. "Or maybe he and Bubba have been so tempted by the smell of my delectable duck dishes that they couldn't take being vegetarians anymore. Maybe they took Zork and…"

All of a sudden, Stevie's face turned as red as a lobster, like he was going to cry.

"Come on," I said. "Let's go talk to Dad."

Lobster is one of the few ingredients I didn't put in my bouillabaisse. Not that I object to lobster or anything. It's just that the ones at the market aren't too perky. I figured I could make do with the traditional prawns and crabs and cheaper fishes, which would make Faarooq happy.

I handed Stevie off to Dad and went back into the kitchen. I had things pretty under control, but after last night, I wanted to be extra ready. Besides, I really didn't feel like poking all over the hotel looking for a stupid duck.

It really doesn't matter whether you put lobster in bouillabaisse or not. The key ingredient is the saffron. That and the orange zest. Just for the heck of it, I decided to add a few chili peppers as well. I figured it'd worked for the mangled eared market guy.

I don't always use wine in my bouillabaisse, though I am tonight. Sometimes it's a problem for me to get wine, on account of my being a minor. No biggie.

It's actually harder for me to get decent lobsters around here than it is for me to get wine. All I really have to do to get wine is go around the corner to the off-track betting parlor. Not that I would, unless I needed it for cooking, and then my mom will usually buy it for me. She says the alcohol burns off in the cooking, so it's fine with her.

The off-track betting parlor doesn't give a rip about selling alcohol to minors, just so long as we don't try and place a bet. They're very strict about their gambling policies.

Another thing you can't get around here is good salami. I don't know why, but you just can't. The market carries all sorts of good caviar and truffles and gourmet stuff like that, but its salami isn't worth a crap.

Speaking of crap, Zork turned up just before we opened the dining room. It was actually Scout who tracked him down. The dumb bird was trapped inside the air duct.

A duck in a duct.

"What's with that stupid bird always getting stuck in chutes?" I said to Stevie.

"He's probably having flashbacks from your hallucinogenic wheat," he said.

"Yeah, right," I said. Next time he's going straight in the pot.

Chapter 12

Don't ask me why, but ever since they got Zork out of the duct, the air in the hotel kitchen has actually been circulating.

It's a miracle.

Don't get me wrong, it still smells like a garbage truck in there, but at least now the smell wafts around the room on gentle currents of air instead of hanging over the stove like a dead duck in the window of a Chinese restaurant.

That's a lovely image, isn't it?

The dinner crowd that evening was not nearly as big as it had been the night before. I guess Scout had been too busy playing cards and looking for Zork to do any serious advertising.

On the bus ride home, Stevie told me that Scout was homesick for Mexico. "He wants to go back and buy a ball park," he said.

"How do you know that?" I asked.

"I just do," he said.

I believed him. Somehow Stevie had found a way to communicate with Scout, and he didn't need a lexicon or anything. They just seemed to understand each other.

Stevie's like that. He can relate to all sorts of people, even the weird ones. Especially the weird ones.

Takes one to know one, I say.

In my Sandy Koufax-Mickey Mantle lexicon, Stevie's name is STEE FIX YUMMY CANADA KLONK.

"What the heck's Canada Klonk?"

"French fries," I said. That's about the only thing my brother can make in the oven, besides frozen pizza and chicken nuggets. French fries are big in Canada, where they serve them with gravy and cheese curds. They call the stuff poutine.

"Sounds gross," said Stevie. I think it's the curds that put him off. Not how they taste, but the word itself. It sounds too close to something you'd fish out of a toilet.

When I make French fries, I like to serve them with salt and vinegar, the way they do at the beach.

Stevie never gets fries at the beach anymore. He used to get them all the time. Then one day while he was standing in line waiting to be served, he watched the big fat guy behind the counter who was working the deep fryer. The guy was sweating like crazy, Stevie said, and then all of a sudden this big bead of sweat rolled off his face and dripped right into the vat of bubbling oil.

No way was Stevie going to eat something that was cooked in *that*.

Dad explained to Stevie that the French fry oil is super hot, like a thousand degrees or something. He said that all the sweat germs would be killed at that temperature, but it didn't matter to Stevie. He wasn't going to eat those things ever again.

Even though it kind of grosses me out too, I can still eat beach fries since I didn't actually see the fat guy sweating in the grease. One drop of sweat isn't so bad. It'd be different if he'd hocked a big slimy loogy in it.

Scout wasn't from the beachy part of Mexico, though he told Stevie that the beaches there were nice.

Imagine the sweat that must pour off the fries guys down there.

"Maybe we can send him back there for his birthday," suggested Stevie.

"Back where?" I asked.

"Back to Mexico, Stupid."

"Sure Stevie, whatever you say."

I wondered out loud when Scout's birthday was.

Stevie answered me. "It's the fourth of July."

"That's so weird," I said. Not that I thought it was particularly weird that Scout's birthday fell on a big national holiday. I thought it was weird because my own birthday falls on September 16th, which is the official Independence Day of Mexico.

What a weird coincidence.

I don't usually think about the fact that I was born on Mexico's Independence Day. It's not like I always have to have a piñata on my birthday or anything. It's just something I happened to read in a book, and it kind of stuck in my brain.

I'm not sure I'd want to have my birthday fall on a big holiday in this country.

Stevie's birthday is right before Christmas, and he says it sucks because nobody ever really thinks about his birthday. He says everybody's too busy thinking about Christmas to give a crap about how old he is. And then people give him these dumb combination gifts for both occasions, which he says is a total rip.

I can see his point, I guess.

After what Stevie told me about Scout's wanting to go home to Mexico, I thought I should try to do something nice for his birthday. Bake him a cake, at least.

I was going to make him one of those flag cakes with the strawberries and blueberries and whipped cream and junk, but then I thought that would be putting too much emphasis on the fourth of July, which wasn't the point of the cake.

It's just that you don't generally get too many opportunities to make a flag cake. And Flag Day had already passed.

I ended up making Scout a chocolate mint layer cake. I got the idea one night when I was trying to craft a few more anagrams out of Sandy Koufax and Mickey Mantle. I kept coming up with things that included the words MINTY CAKE.

MINTY ELM CAKE

MINTY MEL CAKE

MINTY LEM CAKE

EL M-MINTY CAKE

In the end, I called it MY LE MINT CAKE.   I thought it sounded kind of French, which is a good thing for a dessert, I think.

Scout seemed to really like it. He ate the entire thing at one sitting.

Scout can really pound the food.

Afterwards, I gave him a special present.

"EGGS ON ICE, JARK," I said as he opened the box.

Scout's eyes bugged out as big as baseballs when he saw the Reggie Jackson card. His mouth curled into a long, thin grin like one of those cartoon cats. For once he didn't flash me the tooth.

The gift was as much for me as it was for Scout. I had been feeling kind of limited just having two names' worth of letters to draw from in our baseball-word-jumble language.   I thought if I could add another name to the mix, it might expand our conversations a little bit.

I thought something with an R would be good. We could have used an H as well, but at the last minute, I lost my bid on eBay for the Lou Gehrig card.

Scout picked up the card and studied it closely. Then he looked at me and said, "A GRECO KING, JES."

His ability to rearrange letters into new phrases was astounding, even if the things he came up with were a little weird. It'd taken me fifteen minutes to put together the EGGS ON ICE thing out of the old right fielder's name.

I'm pretty sure Reggie Jackson wasn't Greek, or a Greco, as Scout would say. He was, however, a big dealer in sports memorabilia. He also owned a chain of car dealerships.

I read somewhere that Reggie Jackson once tried to buy the Anaheim Angels but was outbid by a billionaire Mexican named Arturo Moreno.

Seeing that Scout had ties to Mexican baseball, I asked him, "Ever hear of a guy named Arturo Moreno?"

"MEX-CALIFORNIAN GUY STAGED MY SCENE, KOJAKK!"

I had no idea what he meant by that remark, or if it was supposed to mean anything at all. What got my interest was the word KOJAKK, just like the scrawl on the back of the school bus seat, except with a second K stuck at the end.

Even Scout gets stuck with an extra one from time to time.

I was still thinking about the Kojak coincidence when I got on the city bus to go home that night, so at first I didn't notice the man sitting in the back seat. It was Uncle Rico. He moved up to sit beside me.

"What are you doing out so late?" he asked me.

"I work at the Saint George's," I said.

"That place is a rat-trap," said Uncle Rico.

I asked Uncle Rico where he was coming from. He said he'd been to see the fireworks show downtown. I'd totally forgotten it was the fourth of July.

Somehow I doubted Uncle Rico was at a fireworks display. More likely he'd been to the off-track betting parlor around the corner. According to the neighbors, that's where he made all his money, which he supposedly buried in his yard.

"Was the fireworks show any good?" I asked.

"Actually," he said, "it sucked an egg."

Chapter 13

I figured Uncle Rico picked up the "suck an egg" lingo from the school bus.

He's a terrible driver, by the way. His eyesight is shot, so half the time he has to guess about what color the traffic light is. Plus he never waits for kids to get settled into their seats before he takes off.

One time he sped off before Kenny Cravetz had sat down and knocked the dumb twit off balance. Then he slammed on the brakes all of a sudden at a red light, and Kenny shot forward and hit his head on the bus seat. He bawled like a baby the whole way home.

Mrs. Cravetz threatened to report Uncle Rico to the bus people, but he paid her off. Wonder if he had to dig up one of his holes to do it.

There's a rumor that Uncle Rico is somehow related to that billionaire Mexican who bought the Angels, Arturo Moreno. A cousin or something like that.

Even if he does have all kinds of money, I still feel sorry for Uncle Rico for having to live right next door to the Cravetzes. It's bad enough just living down the street from them.

Speaking of the Cravetzes, Faarooq just hired Belinda to wait tables at the Saint George's.

He's got to be breaking a child labor law somewhere.

As far as the Cravetzes go, Belinda is okay, I guess. She's nothing like her stupid brother, Kenny.

Kenny's been bragging again about his latest card collection. Now he's into Mystic Zeltoid cards. Even though he hasn't been collecting them for half as long as the other kids around here, he has all sorts of rare and expensive cards. One of them – the Mystic Moon Pie – is supposed to be worth about a thousand bucks.

Why is it that the yobs always wind up having the coolest stuff?

Kenny and his family came down to the restaurant on Belinda's first day. They all ordered chicken fingers with a side of fries. Very refined. My special that night was lamb kabobs over garlic couscous. It was delicious, if I do say so myself.

I let Stevie fix the Cravetz's chicken fingers. He sometimes comes down to help me in the kitchen, even though he hardly does anything other than talk to Scout.

I found out how Stevie is able to communicate so well with him. What he does is pretend that it's the old days back in Mexico and he's a Mexican baseball player. All of the things he learns from Scout come out of his pretend conversations about baseball.

As far as I know, Stevie doesn't know a darn thing about baseball. I can't even imagine how those conversations would go.

The day the Cravetz family came to dinner, Scout stayed in his room. Even though they know the old dude's crazy, the Cravetzes are still pretty burned up about Kenny's baseball cards. To tell you the truth, I'm a little surprised they let their daughter come work down here.

Maybe they planted her here as a spy.

After the Cravetzes left, Stevie told me a secret about Scout.

"He still has the Sandy Koufax card," he said.

"No way!" I said. "How do you know?"

"He showed it to me."

YUKKY, MEAN OLD MEXICAN FAST, I thought.

"What about Mickey Mantle?" I asked.

"Up in smoke," said Stevie.

"Are you going to tell Kenny?"

"That jerk?" he said. "Heck no."

Chapter 14

Scout was back hanging out in the kitchen the next night. But Stevie wasn't around. He was too tired from cutting lawns.

Last week Uncle Rico went away and asked Stevie to take care of his yard. I don't know how much he's getting paid, but I bet it's more than I am.

Uncle Rico was going to visit his own Uncle Rico in an old folk's home down in South Bend, Indiana. He didn't say when he was coming back. Sometime in August, I think.

Before he left, Uncle Rico came over and fixed our television. Now it gets two stations – the Food Channel and Court TV.

Stevie makes a big deal about having to take care of both our lawn and Uncle Rico's.

Our lawn's about as big as a shoebox. It takes about ten minutes to cut. Big deal, I told him.

Scout was acting all twitchy again, the way he'd been on the night he passed out the stack of hotel stationary. We've never had as many customers as we had that night. Still, we do get a pretty good stream of people most evenings. Friday nights are the biggest.

It was only Thursday, but there was a decent crowd in the dining room. Belinda and I were working our butts off.

Scout wasn't much help. Like I said, he was kind of twitchy.   As soon as I saw how twitchy he was acting, I hid all the extra spoons.

The reason Scout was so anxious was on account of some rich guy named Harlan McFarlan, who showed up at the restaurant at five minutes to five and requested our best table.

I didn't know we had a best table.

Belinda put him in the booth farthest away from the smelly kitchen.

I don't know anything about this Harlan McFarlan guy, except that he's as fat as a house and he made Scout twitchy.   That, and that he isn't particularly big on calamari. His complimentary plate of appetizers came back untouched.

Some people just can't deal with food that has tentacles.

Tentacles.

Another word you don't hear too much, unless you're a marine biologist.

Then there's that other body part that sounds a lot like tentacles which people are pretty squeamish about eating. That I can understand.

Even though he didn't go for the squid, Harlan McFarlan seemed to enjoy the entrée I made for him. It was stuffed pork chops topped with homemade salsa. He polished off the entire plate. He even ate the parsley garnish.

Then he left Belinda a hundred dollar tip. She nearly fainted.

She offered to split the money with me, but I told her to keep it. I feel kind of sorry for her, what with having to put up with Kenny for a brother.

I don't put nearly as many chili peppers in my salsa as the market guy, but it's still pretty darn hot.

Dad told me that this Harlan McFarlan was some big real estate developer from New York City. He said he was planning to buy up everything on the block and tear it down so he could build a bunch of fancy strip malls.

That'll be the end of Dad's cushy job at the old Shanghai.

And Scout will be out on his ear.

I guess that would make me a little twitchy too.

After that night, all anyone could talk about was this Harlan McFarlan fellow. There were even a few stories about him in the paper.

I have to say, he was much fatter in person than he was in the newspaper. Those pictures must have been taken before he'd gorged himself on pork chops.

Then one day something happened that took everyone's mind off the fat New Yorker.

The weird guy from the market was arrested for trying to hold up the Gas 'n Go. Get this – his weapon was a zucchini!

The market guy was wearing a mask when he did it, but the attendant at the gas station recognized him. With his spiky orange hair and half an ear, he's kind of hard to miss.

"I told you he was the Eggplant Cowboy," said Stevie when he heard the news.

"He's not the Eggplant Cowboy, you doofus. He used a zucchini. Besides, if the market guy was the Eggplant Cowboy, don't you think somebody at the hotel would have recognized him?"

"He was wearing a hat," said Stevie. "Jeez, Finch. Sometimes you are so dense."

Hat or no hat, I still don't think the market guy is the Eggplant Cowboy. Either way, I guess I'm going to have to find a new place to shop for groceries.

Chapter 15

Good news. The market guy's back in business. Temporarily, anyway.

He's out on bail. Get this – he was released into the custody of Harlan McFarlan, the big shot from New York.

At first everyone was saying that this Harlan McFarlan was the market guy's long lost father. But he isn't. He's just an opportunistic fat guy from the big city who knows how to wheel and deal.

In return for springing him, Mangled Ear agreed to sell his market to Harlan McFarlan at a good price.

I don't think the deal becomes official for a couple of weeks, which works out okay for me. That'll keep me going with crappy salami and half-thawed imported fish until almost the end of summer. Also fresh baked bread, though generally speaking, I stay away from the Rice and Grains section of that place after the wheat incident.

A couple of police officers stopped by the hotel after Mangled Ear was released.   They told Dad and Faarooq that the Gas 'n Go robbery was a copycat crime.   They were pretty sure the weird spiky-haired guy from the market was not the Eggplant Cowboy.

"What'd I tell you?"

Stevie punched me in the arm.

The policemen stayed around for dinner.   One of them had a PBJ.   The other had a salad.

Belinda rolled her eyes.   "Big spenders," she said.

They were still there when who should walk through the door but Harlan McFarlan.   Belinda's face got all flush, and she kept trying to iron out her apron with her hands.   She's kind of cute when she's nervous.

Harlan McFarlan didn't come to eat this time, though. He was there to try to buy the Saint George's.

Dad left his post and joined Stevie and me in the kitchen.   Scout was in his room, where he'd been lying low since the police arrived.

Dad started pacing back and forth by the back door.   I could see he was upset.   At least he knew enough to stay away from my stove.

I suppose I should be worried for Dad. I mean, it'll suck if he loses his job. But for some reason, I'm not so worried about that.

It's Scout I'm worried about. What's he going to do if they close the Saint George's? He doesn't even have enough money for bus fare back to Mexico. At least, that's what Stevie says.

Of course, if Dad loses his job, it could be my butt out on the street.

I'd have to quit school and get a full-time job.

I'd become a famous teenage chef.

I'd move into my own apartment. One with a plasma television right in the kitchen.

Babes would love me.

Maybe Belinda Cravetz would come over and hang out once in a while. When I wasn't hanging out with all the other hot babes, that is.

I'd let Stevie come by once a week to cut my lawn.

Scratch that. I wouldn't have a lawn if I lived in an apartment.

What kind of famous teenage chef lives in an apartment?

I'd live in a condo.

On the beach. Next to a French fry stand.

Again, without a lawn.

Stevie says lawns are a pain in the butt. Especially lawns next to the Cravetz house.

The Cravetzes don't do anything to take care of their yard. They've got crab grass growing everywhere. It's as out of control as Uncle Rico's hair. Naturally, it all spreads to Uncle Rico's lawn, where Stevie has to root it out.

"Why don't you just use a spray?" I asked.

"I can't," said Stevie. "Suppose Zork gets a hold of it and is poisoned?"

We can only hope.

"You're not really pulling crab grass," I said. "You're just looking for Uncle Rico's buried money."

Stevie didn't say anything.

"So have you found any?" I asked.

"Nah," he finally said.

It's not really the crab grass that irks Stevie. It's Kenny Cravetz. He always comes out to watch Stevie work on Uncle Rico's lawn. He just sits there on his stoop and stares at him. Except for the one time when he stayed hidden in the living room because he had planted plastic forks all over Uncle Rico's yard.

I still don't see what's so funny about that.

Stevie gathered up all the forks and gave them to the market guy that afternoon. "For samples," he told him.

The market guy seemed genuinely touched. The next day when I stopped in, there was a little plate of fried zucchini by the register. It was all cut up into bite-sized pieces. Next to the plate was a sign that said:

Home Grown

Try Some

Beside the sign lay a pile of plastic forks. Some of them still had clumps of dirt on them from Uncle Rico's lawn.

Chapter 16

Stevie got a letter from Uncle Rico saying that he was delayed, and would Stevie mind looking after the yard a little while longer.

There was no return address on the envelope, so Stevie had no way to tell him no even if he'd wanted to.

Along with the letter, Uncle Rico had enclosed a check for a thousand dollars, as well as an autographed picture of the man who holds the record for the most hours of consecutive television watching.

"So are you going to keep doing it?" I asked.

"Guess so," said Stevie. A thousand dollars is a fairly good incentive for a twerpy kid. That week he went down to Uncle Rico's two days ahead of schedule.

When he got down there, he discovered that the lawn mower was out of gas.

Stevie didn't feel like coming back to our house to refill the tank, figuring that Uncle Rico probably had a gas can of his own somewhere around his place. He let himself into Uncle Rico's garage to look for one.

There was no gas can anywhere to be found, but he did discover a rumpled purple mask. It was sitting on a shelf right next to a cowboy hat.

"Are you saying that Uncle Rico is the Eggplant Cowboy?"

"Looks that way."

"Are you gonna turn him in?"

Stevie didn't answer right away. He was thinking about the thousand dollars, no doubt. "Nah," he finally said.

"What if he's dangerous?"

"I don't know." Stevie took another few seconds to consider this, then he looked at me and said, "Do you think he's dangerous?"

"Not really," I said. "Not anymore than Scout or the market guy."

"Finch?" Stevie said.

"Yeah?"

"Do you think maybe we're hanging out with the wrong crowd?"

"Probably," I said. "But it beats hanging out with Kenny Cravetz."

"Right."

Chapter 17

That afternoon when we got to the Saint George's, guess who was sitting in the lobby having coffee with Scout – Harlan McFarlan.

I tugged at Dad's shirt. He shot me one of those *yeah this doesn't look good but what the hell do you want me to do about it?* looks.

I know it wasn't any of my business, but I kind of dragged toward the kitchen extra slowly so I could catch a little bit of what was going on.

Scout had an envelope in his hand. He handed it over to Harlan McFarlan, and I heard him say, "SKY OF XANADU."

"Ah man," I said to myself. "He's selling Sandy Koufax." I shook my head and went off to chop onions.

Faarooq was sitting in the kitchen eating leftover eggplant parmesan. It had sort of become one of our signature dishes after the attempted robbery.

"What's up, Saheeb?" he said.

I shrugged. "Not much."

"Oh no, Saheeb, you are wrong. Much is up."

"Oh yeah?" I said. "Like what? You sell the place to that fat New Yorker?"

Faarooq's mouth stretched into that coy, tight-lipped grin of his. "That's right, Saheeb." He ate another forkful of eggplant parmesan and popped off the counter stool. "You are looking at a rich man."

"Great," I said. "So, uh, what exactly does that mean?"

Faarooq gave a little bow and started walking toward the door. "It means that tonight you are cooking your last meal for the Saint George's."

"Oh, well all right," I said to the back of the swinging door.

I wish I had known this was going to be my last dinner. I would have planned something a little more exciting than turkey ragout.

I popped in my old *Dark Side of the Moon* CD by Pink Floyd and cranked up the volume to *Money*. Belinda says she likes Pink Floyd, which is pretty cool for a girl. Stevie used to run around the house singing their song that goes, "We don't need no education," until Mom made him shut-up.

I was humming along to *Money* and didn't hear Dad come through the swinging door.

"Looks like we're out on our butts," he said, taking a seat at the counter where Faarooq had just been sitting.

"What are you gonna do?" I asked.

"I don't know," he said. "I was hoping you might have an idea."

I had no idea.

I couldn't think of anything besides the fact that Pink Floyd wasn't really the greatest accompaniment for turkey ragout. Then Scout burst through the door. He was waving around a wad of cash.

"You sold Kenny's Sandy Koufax, didn't you?" I said.

He slapped the wad on the counter. I picked it up and counted. "Two-eighty," I said. "Not bad." I had no idea if two-hundred-and-eighty dollars was a good deal or not for a Sandy Koufax. Either way, it was probably enough to get him back to Mexico.

"So I guess you'll be heading home soon?" I said.

"U ASK FOXY DAN," he said, giving a nod toward my father.

I looked at my Dad slumped over the counter. Foxy Dan was choking on a piece of eggplant parmesan.

Chapter 18

At midnight that night, the Saint George's hotel officially closed for good. Dad helped me pack up a few things from the kitchen, then we said good-bye to Faarooq and Bubba.

Faarooq shook my hand. "Good luck, Saheeb," he said. Boo-boo just gave a little wave and bowed her head.

I have no idea what they plan to do now. I don't suppose we'll ever hear from them again.

As for Scout, he came home with us.

I can't believe I didn't see that one coming.

Stevie gave up his bed for Scout and moved into my room. Naturally, he brought Zork with him.

After just one night, my entire collection of Julia Child cookbooks was covered in duck crap.

Dad didn't go to bed at all that night. He just sat in his Lazy-Boy watching Court TV until the sun came up.

"Don't worry, Dad," I said the next morning. "Something'll turn up."

I made him eggs benedict for breakfast.

"Anyway," I said as I poured him a glass of fresh squeezed orange juice, "Stevie has a thousand dollars. We can use that if things get tight."

Stevie glared at me, but he didn't say anything. He didn't want to upset Dad anymore than I did. Either that or he was afraid that if he said something stupid, I'd snuff the duck.

"Where's Scout?" I asked after Stevie had taken a couple bites of his breakfast.

"Mowing Uncle Rico's lawn," he said with his mouth stuffed full of eggs. Some of the sauce dribbled down his chin.

"You're making Scout mow your lawns? That's so lame."

"I'm helping him earn a little more money so he can go home," said Stevie. "The sale from the Sandy Koufax card won't quite cover his expenses."

"How much is a bus ride to Mexico?" I asked.

Stevie's face was covered in egg yolk and sauce. He was almost as disgusting to look at as the mangled eared market guy. "Close to three-hundred, I think."

"Oh." I couldn't stand it any longer. I grabbed a rag from the sink and threw it at Stevie's face. "Wipe your face."

Stevie must have still been savoring the hollandaise sauce because he didn't give me any crap. He just did what I asked and wiped the rag around the rim of his mouth.

"So what are you paying Scout to mow Uncle Rico's lawn?" I asked.

"Five dollars," he said. "Six if he weeds out the crab grass."

"You're so cheap," I said.

"Hey, he offered to do it for free."

"Yeah, right."

"Seriously," said Stevie.

I went to the window and looked down the street toward Uncle Rico's house. Scout was on his hands and knees, obviously digging holes in the lawn. He was wearing Uncle Rico's cowboy hat.

"You told him there was money out there, didn't you?"

Stevie shrugged.

"You're so lame."

Dad pushed away from the table and went back to his Lazy-Boy. He hadn't touched a bite of his eggs benedict. Stevie grabbed his plate. I figured he would polish off Dad's too, but he didn't. Instead he put it on the floor and fed it to Zork.

"Man, Stevie," I said. "That duck's gonna crap everywhere now."

Stevie got up and followed Dad into the living room. "Whatever."

I cleaned up the breakfast dishes and went outside to sit on the stoop. Mom had gotten up early and was working in the garden.

"What's gonna happen now that Dad's lost his job?" I asked her.

"I don't know," she said. "Maybe I'll plant zucchinis and we can become bank robbers."

Everybody's a comedian.

I walked down the street to talk to Scout. There were little piles of wilted crab grass everywhere.

"I really don't think there's any money buried around here," I said.

Scout pushed up the brim of his cowboy hat. "ENEMY MUD YAX KNOCK IS FATAL," he said.

Enemy Mud Yax would be Harlan McFarlan. "Yeah, I know it sucks that they closed the Saint George's."

Scout nodded and went back to his work. Watching him up close, I realized that he was mostly just pulling crab grass. He worked super fast, too. It's those quick hands.

"Stevie's not paying you enough," I said.

Scout glanced up. "ME KICK A FAMOUS TEXAN, LYNDY."

I smiled. That one was straight out of my original lexicon. The first edition, before Reggie Jackson was added. What it meant was *Don't worry. I can take care of myself.*

"How much money do you need?" I asked.

"JINKY! NEED SIX K FOR GAME LOT. ME SNAG A YUCCA, K?"

He leaned down and ripped out a clump of crab grass.

I smirked. "Six K," I said, taking the weed from him. "Jinky."

Chapter 19

"So Scout's really planning to buy a ball field?" I asked Stevie when I went back inside.

"That's the plan," he said.

"And he needs six-thousand dollars?" I asked.

"More or less."

"And you're paying him five dollars to weed Uncle Rico's lawn?"

"Six," he said. "Would you move. You're blocking the television."

I stepped to the side. For Dad's sake, not Stevie's.

"Where's today's paper?" I asked.

"Why?" said Stevie.

"I'm gonna look for a job."

Stevie snorted. "It's in the kitchen," he said. "Knock yourself out."

The newspaper was in the kitchen, just like Stevie'd said. It was spread all over the floor, covered in duck crap.

"Stink-ox!" I said loud enough for Stevie to hear.

"What did I tell you about your language, Atticus?"

Guess my mother heard it too. Apparently, she knows the code.

Mothers.

I went to my room and got my paycheck.

"I'm going to cash my check and get a paper," I said to Dad as I walked out the front door.

"Pick up a couple of those summer squash while you're at it," called my mom from the side of the house.

"Yeah, right," I said.

I thought about swiping the paper lying on the Cravetz's lawn, but then I figured Belinda might want to look for a job too. Besides, I still needed to cash my paycheck.

I walked down to the Gas 'n Go and bought a paper. At the last minute, I threw in one of those packs of baseball cards that come with a stick of stale bubble gum that tastes like cardboard.

There were five cards in the pack and one stick of sweet pink cardboard.

Four of the cards were guys I'd never heard of. The fifth was a Barry Bonds – the guy who used steroids to go after Babe Ruth's home run record.

I popped the gum into my mouth and shoved the cards in my pant's pocket.

I walked outside and headed for the bank across the street, but at the last minute I changed my mind and kept on going. I was feeling very impulsive for some reason.

I walked for the next hour or so until I had walked all the way into town.

By the time I got there, I was sweating like a pig.

I really don't know what made me do that. I guess I just wanted to take one last look at everything before Harlan McFarlan turned it into a giant strip mall.

I cashed my check at the off-track betting parlor around the corner from the Saint George's. I tried to place a bet, but they wouldn't let me. I was too young, they said.

I don't get why that matters.

As I was walking home, I saw the orange-haired guy from the market sitting by a grate. Next to him was a plate of fried zucchini pieces with a bunch of dirty forks stuck in them. In front of it was a hat with a sign propped on it:

Home Grown

Try Some

50¢ a piece

Actually, it wasn't so much of a hat as a cap. A ratty wool ski cap, which drooped to the side like a wilted flower. I leaned down and shoved my baseball cards into it along with twenty bucks.

"I don't want any zucchini," I said, "but it'd be great if you could put some of this on Foxy Dan in the fourth race for me. If it comes in, I'll split the winnings with you."

Mangled Ear didn't even look at me. He just snatched the money out of the cap and put it in his pocket. Then he popped a zucchini into his mouth.

I knew he wasn't the Eggplant Cowboy.

Can you believe there was actually a horse called Foxy Dan?

Chapter 20

When I got home, Dad was sitting on the front stoop by the fu dog looking numbly content.

It wasn't natural.

I think it's the first time in twenty years that my father has been in direct contact with real sunlight. I stood there on the walkway just watching him for a minute.

When he didn't burn up like a vampire, I went up to him.

"What's up with you?" I asked.

"Stevie got a letter from Uncle Rico," he said.

"Oh yeah? He coming home soon?"

Dad shook his head. "He said he's gonna be away for a while. A year maybe."

"He's on the lamb," I said. "He's the Eggplant Cowboy, you know."

"No," said Dad. "I didn't know that."

"So why do you have that dumb expression on your face? And why are you sitting out here in the sun?"

"I got a job," he said. Then he got up and went back inside the house.

Dad's job is to keep an eye on Uncle Rico's house at night while he's away. Uncle Rico promised to pay him whatever they paid him at the Saint George's.

So basically now Dad will get paid just for sitting in his own Lazy-Boy all night. And he can watch Court TV while he works.

Sweet.

Stevie's job was also extended. He didn't seem to mind as much as I thought he would. Why would he? Scout was doing most of the work for him now anyway. It didn't hurt that Uncle Rico had advanced him another couple thousand.

No sooner had Dad started his job as Uncle Rico's night watchman than there was a robbery in the neighborhood.

It wasn't Uncle Rico's place.

It was the Cravetz's.

Somebody had broken in and snatched a bunch of Kenny's Mystic Zeltoid cards.

"Did you see who did it?" my mother asked Dad the next morning at breakfast.

Dad just grunted.

We all knew who did it, of course.

Scout was nowhere to be found.

Later when it was just Stevie and me, I asked my brother about him. "Is he gone for good?"

"What do you think?" he said.

Stevie wasn't really in the mood for conversation right then. He was too busy admiring the Mystic Moon Pie card he'd discovered under the fu dog when he went to get the paper.

Stevie wasn't really into Mystic Zeltoid cards anymore. What he was into was money.

I have to admit, he had quite a collection of it.

A week later he sold the Mystic Moon Pie card to some whacko on eBay. Get this – the person he sold it to was named T. Fairy.

By the time Labor Day rolled around, my little brother was practically a millionaire.

"When school starts, you should probably keep your trap shut about how rich you are," I said. "We don't need our house getting robbed."

"Oh yeah, right." Stevie rolled his eyes at me. "Who do you think's gonna rob it? Both Scout and Uncle Rico are probably out of the country."

"The mangled ear guy from the market's still lurking around."

"Our dad's a night watchman, Finch. Nobody's gonna try and break into our house."

"Yeah, I guess," I said. "Still, it's too bad we don't have the other fu dog." To be honest, I agreed with Stevie. I didn't really think anyone would try to rob us. Especially not the market guy, although he does know where we live.

Believe it or not, he actually mailed me a hundred bucks. It was from the horse race.

Foxy Dan won.

The odds had been three-hundred-to-one. Mangled Ear made six-thousand dollars out of the twenty I'd given him.

Nice of him to share the profits with me.

I used my winnings to buy some very expensive steaks for dinner.

I don't really miss cooking for the restaurant at the Saint George's. It was a good experience, I guess, but I'm glad to be making dinner in my own kitchen again.

It's a heck of a lot easier to cook for just Mom, Dad and Stevie than for ten or forty or seventy-seven people. Plus our house doesn't smell like a garbage truck.

Of course, there is duck crap everywhere.

Chapter 21

As we were walking to the bus stop on that first day back to school, I got to thinking about Uncle Rico and how he wouldn't be around this year to drive the bus if they needed him.

I wondered if we'd have to walk to school when the regular bus driver called in sick.

Thinking about Uncle Rico's being gone got me thinking about Scout as well. As we climbed onto the bus driven by the person who wasn't Uncle Rico, I said to Stevie, "I wonder if Scout ever got enough money to buy his ball field."

"He did," said Stevie.

"How do you know? Did you hear from him?"

Stevie pointed to the seat in front of me as I slid in to take my usual spot.

The words KOJAK SUCKS AN EGG were still there scribbled in blue marker. Only now, something else was written beneath them: RELAX TC.   I FIND MY MONEY. E.A.

Stevie sat down beside me. Neither of us said anything the whole way to school.

We hardly talked about Scout after that. I guess we just got busy with other things and kind of forgot about all the past junk from last summer.

Then right after Stevie's birthday, a Christmas card arrived. It was a picture of Scout waving from the middle of a sunny baseball diamond. If you squinted, you could just make out the other fu dog sitting behind the backstop. I showed it to Stevie.

"Look who's standing next to him," I said.

Stevie grinned back at the smiling faces of Uncle Rico and the market guy.

"What do you know about that," he said.

Inside the card it said, TICKY NOEL – MAKE X-MAS DAY FUN!

Stevie laid the card on the coffee table and followed me into the kitchen.

"So what are you making tonight, Finch?"

I wiped a bunch of crap off the bottom of my shoe. "I'm roasting your duck," I said.

"Stink-ox," said Stevie.

"TICKY NOEL," I said.

www.ingramcontent.com/pod-product-compliance
Lightning Source LLC
Chambersburg PA
CBHW021003150626
46549CB00012BA/992